FROGGY'S BABY SISTER

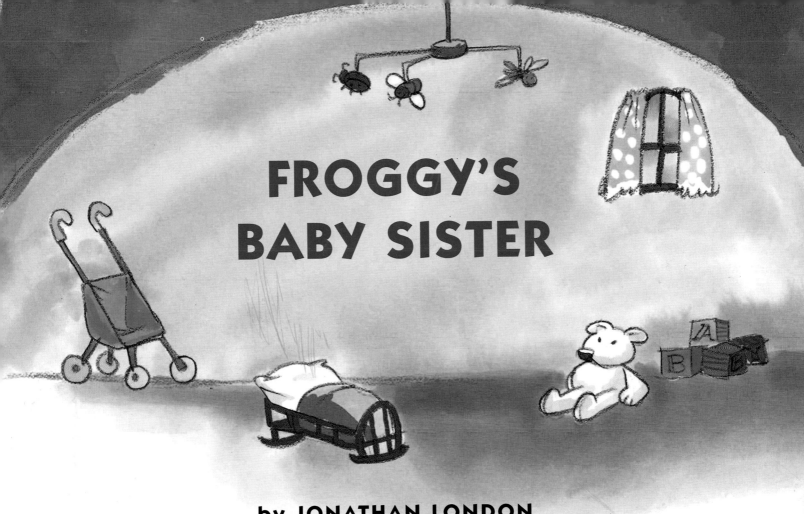

FROGGY'S BABY SISTER

by JONATHAN LONDON

illustrated by FRANK REMKIEWICZ

PUFFIN BOOKS

For Aaron & Sean;
and for sweet Maureen & Regina—both great at what they do
   —J. L.

For Debby of Circle Books,
the most frequent flyer in the Froggy costume
   —F. R.

PUFFIN BOOKS
Published by the Penguin Group
Penguin Young Readers Group, 345 Hudson Street, New York, New York 10014, U.S.A.
Penguin Group (Canada), 10 Alcorn Avenue, Toronto, Ontario, Canada M4V 3B2 (a division of Pearson Penguin Canada Inc.)
Penguin Books Ltd, 80 Strand, London WC2R 0RL, England
Penguin Ireland, 25 St Stephen's Green, Dublin 2, Ireland (a division of Penguin Books Ltd)
Penguin Group (Australia), 250 Camberwell Road, Camberwell, Victoria 3124, Australia (a division of Pearson Australia Group Pty Ltd)
Penguin Books India Pvt Ltd, 11 Community Centre, Panchsheel Park, New Delhi - 110 017, India
Penguin Group (NZ), Cnr Airborne and Rosedale Roads, Albany, Auckland 1310, New Zealand (a division of Pearson New Zealand Ltd)
Penguin Books (South Africa) (Pty) Ltd, 24 Sturdee Avenue, Rosebank, Johannesburg 2196, South Africa
Registered Offices: Penguin Books Ltd, 80 Strand, London WC2R 0RL, England

First published in the United States of America by Viking, a division of Penguin Young Readers Group, 2003
Published by Puffin Books, a division of Penguin Young Readers Group, 2005

20 19 18 17 16 15 14

THE LIBRARY OF CONGRESS HAS CATALOGED THE VIKING EDITION AS FOLLOWS:
London, Jonathan, date–
Froggy's baby sister / by Jonathan London ; illustrated by Frank Remkiewicz.
p.   cm.
Summary: Froggy hoped for a brother to play with so he is disappointed with his new baby sister,
Pollywogilina, but only until she is old enough to start learning from her big brother.
ISBN 0-670-03659-5 (hc)
[1. Babies—Fiction. 2. Brothers and sisters—Fiction. 3. Frogs—Fiction.]
I. Remkiewicz, Frank, ill. II. Title.
PZ7.L8432Frv 2003   [E]—dc21   2003000950

Puffin Books ISBN 978-0-14-240342-6

Manufactured in China
Set in Kabel

Froggy woke up.
"Is this the big day?" he wondered.
He hopped out of bed
and flopped to the kitchen—*flop flop flop.*

"Good morning, Froggy," said his mother.
"Wow, Mom!" said Froggy. "Your tummy is *huge*!
Is the baby coming today?"

"I hope so!"
She patted her belly and beamed.
"I want a baby brother!" said Froggy.
"Sisters are great, too," said his mom.

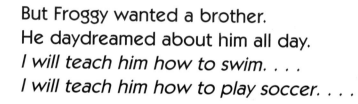

But Froggy wanted a brother.
He daydreamed about him all day.
I will teach him how to swim. . . .
I will teach him how to play soccer. . . .

FRROOGGYY!

called his father.
"Wha-a-a-at?"
"I'm taking Mom to the hospital!
Max's mother will stay with you."

And off they zoomed in a taxicab.
Froggy felt like he'd swallowed
dragonflies for lunch.

Max's mother tried to read to him,
but Froggy couldn't sit still.
She tried to play catch with him . . .
but he kept falling flat on his face—*oof!*
When will the baby come? he wondered.

Finally he dozed off under the kitchen table.

FRROOGGYY!

called his father.
"Wha-a-a-t?"
"Come see the baby!"

Froggy jumped up
and hit his head on the table—*bonk!*—
then flopped to the baby's room—
flop flop flop.

"It's a girl!" said Froggy's dad.
"A *girl*?" cried Froggy. *"Yuck!"*
"Her name is Pollywogilina!" said Mom.
"But you can call her Polly for short."

WAAAAAAAAA!

cried Polly.
"Maybe she's hungry!" said Froggy.
"Let's make her burgers and flies!"

Soon, Polly was sitting on Mommy's lap sucking on a bottle of cream of fly mush—*slurp slurp slurp.*

"Let *me* feed her!" said Froggy.
"I can take care of her all by myself!"
"Not yet," said Froggy's mom.
"When her legs are all grown in
and she loses her tail—
then you can take care of her."

Spring ended. Summer came.
Froggy wanted to teach Polly how to bounce
on a pogo stick—*boing! boing! boing!*
But Polly was too little.

He wanted to teach her how to
jump off a swing.
But Polly was too little.
"You can't do *anything*!" he said.
And he flew off the swing . . .

and landed in the pond—*splash!*

One day, Frogilina came to see the baby.
"She's cute!" said Frogilina.
"Hey, let's play Mommy and Daddy!"
"No way!" cried Froggy.
And he flopped away—*flop flop flop.*

Summer was almost over.
"I'm tired of waiting!" said Froggy.
"Polly's no fun.
I'm going over to Max's
and I'm never coming back!"

FRROOGGYY!

called his mom.
"What-a-a-a-t?"
"Wait!"
Mom unwrapped Polly's blanket.

"Legs!" cried Froggy.
"And her tail's all gone!
Yippee! Now can I take care of her?"
"Yes," said Mom.
"Here's her diaper bag."

As soon as Mom went inside,
Polly began to cry—
"W-A-A-A-A-A-A-A-A-A-A-A!"
"I know!" said Froggy. "You're *hungry*!"
So he sat her down by the pond
and said, "Watch me!"

And Froggy snagged three flies—*zap! zap! zap!*

Polly flicked her tongue out, too . . .
and caught her first fly—*zap!*
"That's pretty good," said Froggy,
"for a girl!"

"W-A-A-A-A-A-A-A-A-A-A-A!"
"I know!" said Froggy,
and sniffed her diapers—
zniff! zniff! zniff!

"*Yikes!*" cried Froggy,
holding his nose.
"Pollywogilina! You *stink!*"

So he lay Polly down
on her back
and tore off her diaper—
rrrrriiiipppp!

Then Froggy wrestled a new diaper on.

FRROOGGYY! called his mom.
"Wha-a-a-t?"
"Time to come in!"
Froggy flopped inside with Polly—
flop flop flop.

"Guess what, Mom," said Froggy.
"I taught Polly how to catch flies!
And I put her diaper on—
all by myself!"
Froggy lifted Polly up and . . .
zloop!—off fell her diaper!
"Oops!" cried Froggy,
looking more red in the face
than green.

That night, Polly wouldn't go to sleep.

WAAAAAAAAA!

She cried and cried.
"Fwo . . . Fwo . . . Fwo . . .
FWWWOOGGYY!"
wailed Polly.

So Froggy flopped to Polly's cradle—
flop flop flop—and picked her up.
"She misses her big brother," said Froggy.
"Go to sleep, Pollywogilina!"

And Polly went to sleep
in Froggy's arms.
ZZZZZZZZZZZZZZ.